Ho

S uddenly Ne⬛⬛⬛⬛⬛⬛⬛⬛⬛ e snow ahead of him, directly in his path. He squinted through the snowflakes, trying to work out what it was. Then he realized, and his heart lurched. It was a Labrador puppy and, from what he could see, it was not very old.

"Look out!" Neil yelled. Frantically, he dug his heels into the snow, trying to slow his descent, but the sledge swept on, as fast as ever, and the puppy didn't move. It watched, wide-eyed with apprehension, as Neil sped towards it . . .

Titles in the Puppy Patrol® *series*

More Puppy Patrol® stories to follow soon

Puppy Patrol®
Holly's Wish

Jenny Dale

Illustrated by

Mick Reid

A Working Partners Book

MACMILLAN CHILDREN'S BOOKS

Special thanks to Liss Norton

First published 2000 by Macmillan Children's Books
a division of Macmillan Publishers Limited
25 Eccleston Place, London SW1W 9NF
Basingstoke and Oxford
www.macmillan.com

Associated companies throughout the world

Created by Working Partners Limited
London W6 0QT

ISBN 0 330 48411 7

1 3 5 7 9 8 6 4 2

A CIP catalogue record for this book is available from
the British Library.

Typeset in Bookman Old Style by SX Composing DTP, Rayleigh, Essex
Printed and bound in Great Britain by Mackays of Chatham plc, Kent

Chapter One

"**C**ome on, Jake!" Neil Parker called to his young black-and-white Border collie as he tramped through the snow to the top of the ridgeway. He stopped to look back, and laughed at Jake's antics. The young dog was racing to and fro, trying to catch the whirling snowflakes in his mouth. Below them lay the snowy roofs of the small country town of Compton.

"Hurry up!" Emily, Neil's ten-year-old sister, called impatiently from further up the slope. "At this rate the snow will have melted before we get to the top."

Neil laughed. "There's not much chance of that," he said as he ran to catch up with her,

1

dragging his sledge behind him. Neil had woken up that morning to find a carpet of deep snow covering the yard and roof-tops of King Street Kennels, the dog kennels and rescue centre that his parents, Bob and Carole Parker, ran. It had continued to snow steadily all morning and Neil hoped it would last until Christmas, which was only a week away.

He gazed up at the sky, narrowing his eyes against the dancing flakes, then smiled with satisfaction. The clouds looked heavy and grey, and Neil was sure there was still plenty of snow to come.

"Come on!" Emily called again. "Everyone else is there already. We don't want to miss all the fun." She turned and hurried up the hill with her sledge, her feet sinking into the snow at every step.

Neil whistled for Jake, then followed Emily, scanning the hillside above as he walked. It was crowded with sledgers and, even from this distance, Neil could identify quite a few of them. Chris Wilson and Hasheem Lindon, Neil's best friends from school, were trudging along the top of the ridgeway with a sledge. Toby and Amanda Sparrow were there too, with their young Dalmatian, Scrap. Steve Tansley, Neil's cousin, was involved in a snowball fight with a group of friends while his wayward Labrador, Ricky, charged backwards and forwards through the snow, barking with excitement.

"Look at Ben," Emily giggled as they climbed. "There's more snow on his coat than there is on the ground." Ben was an Old English sheepdog who belonged to Emily's best friend, Julie.

Neil grinned, then looked back at Jake again. The collie had almost caught up with them and his fur was caked in snow too. "Here, Jake," Neil called, crouching down. "You look like a snow dog!"

Jake hurtled towards him, sending flurries of loose snow flying up behind him. He cannoned into Neil, knocking him over. "Get off!" chuckled Neil, gently pushing the collie off him and scrambling to his feet. He caught hold of Jake's collar and brushed the worst of the snow off his coat while the Border collie nuzzled him with his wet nose. Neil gave him a dog treat from the supply he always carried in his pocket and Jake crunched it eagerly. Then the young dog raced ahead up the hill with an excited bark.

"Here's the Puppy Patrol!" called Hasheem as Neil and Emily reached the top of the hill. He grinned at Neil. "Hey, haven't you got a special doggy sledge for Jake to ride on?"

Neil laughed. "He wouldn't bring his own sledge, Hasheem. He wanted to sit on your lap and ride down." He whistled and Jake came bounding up, ready to play.

"No way!" cried Hasheem, backing away in mock terror. Neil scooped up a handful of snow, shaped it into a snowball and threw it at Hasheem. It hit his chest, leaving a snowy mark. Hasheem laughed and hurled one back but his aim was wide of the mark and he hit Chris instead. In moments, a full-scale snowball fight had broken out.

"Is this a private fight or can anyone join in?" asked Julie, running up with Ben at her heels.

"The more, the merrier," laughed Emily, throwing a snowball at Julie then diving out of the way as her friend hurled one back. Ben and Jake dashed around wildly, leaping up to catch the snowballs as they rocketed over their heads.

"Yuck," Chris panted after a while, brushing snow off his clothes so that it showered around his feet. "My gloves are soaked." He peeled them off and shook them out.

"Does anyone want a sledge race?" Emily asked.

"You bet!" Neil whooped.

They all ran to fetch their sledges and positioned them at the top of the slope. Jake and Ben watched with interest, and Neil began to wonder whether Hasheem's suggestion that Jake should have a sledge of his own wasn't such a bad idea after all. The young Border collie would probably enjoy skimming down the hillside faster than he could run.

"Ready, steady, go!" cried Neil, and they pushed off.

"Last one down has to give us all a piggy back

to the top!" Julie shrieked as they raced downhill.

The ridgeway was perfect for tobogganing. The slope was long enough and steep enough to allow sledges to build up speed, but it levelled out at the bottom so that it was easy to stop. As he zoomed down, Neil could hear Jake barking loudly behind him. But the Border collie couldn't keep up with the speeding sledge and when Neil glanced back over his shoulder he saw Jake bounding after Ben instead, in a boisterous game of chase.

Julie reached the bottom of the hill first. Neil arrived a moment later, with Emily close behind him. Chris and Hasheem were last, slowed down because they were sharing a sledge.

"That was ace!" Neil cried, jumping up. "Let's have another go." He grinned at Chris and Hasheem. "Of course, as you two came last you'll have to give us all a piggy back to the top."

"No chance!" Hasheem yelled, darting a little way up hill.

They trailed back to the top of the hill, towing their sledges and talking excitedly about Christmas. Jake and Ben charged over to meet them, barking greetings.

"Come on, Chris," said Hasheem. "If we get

away quickly, we might win this time." He and Chris jumped on to their sledge and shot away. Neil, Emily and Julie quickly pulled their sledges into position. Jake gave an excited bark, then caught the rope of Neil's sledge in his teeth. "Let go, Jake!" Neil said. "Do you want me to be last this time?"

Jake dropped the rope, then raced around Neil's sledge instead. By the time Neil was ready to go, Julie and Emily were already halfway down the hill and Chris and Hasheem were nearly at the bottom. "Typical! Who'd have a dog?" Neil said, ruffling Jake's ears affectionately. Jake wagged his tail furiously and licked Neil's cheek.

"Mind out of the way then, Jake," said Neil, gently shoving the Border collie to one side. He pushed off with his feet and streaked away down the slope.

Suddenly Neil saw a dark shape in the snow ahead of him, directly in his path. He squinted through the snowflakes, trying to work out what it was. Then he realized, and his heart lurched. It was a Labrador puppy and, from what he could see, it was not very old.

"Look out!" Neil yelled. Frantically, he dug his heels into the snow, trying to slow his descent, but the sledge swept on as fast as ever, and the puppy didn't move. It watched, wide-eyed with apprehension, as Neil sped towards it.

Neil hauled on the rope. He had to change direction. If he hit the pup, it would be badly hurt. The nose of the sledge inched round. Neil jerked harder and the sledge swerved to the left.

To his relief, he realized that he was just going to miss the puppy – if it stayed where it was. But now Neil was heading for a prickly holly bush. He jerked on the rope again. This time it was too late. Shutting his eyes and throwing up his arms to protect his face, he hurtled straight into the bush.

Chapter Two

The branches lashed Neil as he barged into the holly bush, their prickly leaves snatching at his clothes. A branch caught in the collar of his coat and he tumbled into the snow.

He lay still for a moment, looking up at the dark glossy leaves and scarlet berries above his head. One of his gloves had been torn off in the crash and there was a long scratch on the back of his hand. Neil flexed his arms and legs, checking that he hadn't broken any bones. Then he rolled over and sat up.

"Neil!" Emily's frightened voice reached him from the bottom of the hill. "Are you all right?"

"Neil!" Chris yelled. "Where are you, mate?"

"Over here," called Neil. "I'm OK." He crawled out of the bush.

Jake hurtled down the slope, sending snow sliding ahead of him. He stood in front of Neil and looked at him enquiringly with his head on one side.

"It's OK, boy," Neil said, hugging the Border collie. "I'm not hurt."

Ben arrived a moment later and flopped down in the snow beside Jake with his tongue lolling. Neil patted him too.

Emily came charging up the hill, her face pink from running, with Chris, Hasheem and Julie close behind. "Are you all right?" she panted anxiously.

"Fine," said Neil as he got to his feet. "Apart from a few scratches and a lost glove, anyway. Is the puppy OK?" The Labrador was still standing above them on the slope, chest-deep in snow. It was watching them with huge brown eyes, its chocolate-brown coat speckled with snowflakes.

Hasheem laughed. "There's nothing wrong with you if you're worrying about dogs again!"

"The puppy looks OK," said Emily. "But why on earth is it on its own?"

"That's what I'd like to know too," Neil said

hotly. "It's too young to be out of doors in weather like this." He set off up the slope towards the puppy, with the others trailing after him. "The poor little thing must be frozen. I'd really like to hear what the owners have got to say about—" He broke off suddenly. "Hang on! Isn't it Holly, one of the Labrador puppies from the litter at the rescue centre? It looks exactly like her. And it's the right size."

"It does look like her," Emily agreed, "though I'm not one hundred per cent sure."

"What, she's one of those tiny puppies that were living in a box in your kitchen for a while?" asked Chris. "I fed one of them once when I came over to your house. It was a little black one."

Neil nodded. "That's right." The Parkers had hand-reared the four tiny Labradors after they had been found abandoned in the woods on the far side of Compton. They were only a few days old when they were rescued, and they had lived in the kitchen until they were big enough to move into the rescue centre.

"I fed them a couple of times too," Julie said. "They were really sweet." She looked at the puppy again. "Are they all as big as this one now?"

11

"One of the black ones, Santa, is a bit smaller," said Neil. He signalled to everyone to slow down as they drew closer to the Labrador pup. It was important to approach her quietly so that they didn't frighten her. He placed a restraining hand on Jake's collar. "Can you hang on to Ben, Julie?" he asked.

Julie grabbed hold of the Old English sheepdog.

"Someone left the puppies to die," Emily explained to Hasheem. "The owner dumped them in a bag in the middle of nowhere."

"That's terrible!" said Hasheem angrily. "What an awful thing to do!"

"They could easily have died of cold," Emily went on, with a shiver.

"Or starvation," Neil added gravely.

"I can't imagine anyone being that cruel," said Chris.

"We don't get many cases as bad as that," Emily said. "And luckily the puppies were found quite quickly by a man who was out walking his dog. He brought them straight to King Street Kennels."

"The Puppy Patrol to the rescue again!" Hasheem said. "What on earth would dogs do without the Parkers and their rescue centre?"

"Wait here now," Neil said over his shoulder. "The puppy will be scared if we all get too close." He clipped on Jake's lead and thrust it into Emily's hand. "Stay, Jake," he told the Border collie. Then he edged forward cautiously so that the Labrador wouldn't run off. "Holly," he called softly.

"Holly! Very appropriate," Hasheem joked, "seeing as you've just wrecked a holly bush, Neil, with your crazy sledge run."

They all started to laugh but Neil turned and placed a warning finger on his lips. "Don't scare her," he whispered, and the laughter quickly died away. "Holly," Neil called again. "Here, Holly. Good girl."

At the sound of her name, the Labrador puppy pricked up her ears and wagged her tiny tail feebly.

"I *knew* it was her," said Neil.

"Julie and I will fetch the sledges while you get hold of Holly," Emily said. "We'll take Jake and Ben with us, just in case they bother her. Come on, you two, let's go," she called to the dogs.

Holly watched Neil with a trusting expression as he advanced. At last he was close enough to touch her. He reached out a hand, letting her sniff his bare skin, then he lifted her into his arms. "Good girl," he said soothingly.

The puppy snuggled against him, shivering. "Poor thing, you're frozen," said Neil, brushing snow off Holly's glossy coat. She was wearing a red leather collar with an identity disc. Neil twisted the collar round until he could read the disc. The name *Morgan* was inscribed on it, with a telephone number underneath.

"Is it definitely Holly?" Chris asked, moving forward and holding out his hand to the young Labrador. She craned forward to sniff him, then sank back against Neil's chest again, with a weary sigh.

"Yes." Neil unzipped his coat and tucked the shivering pup inside. "It says Morgan on her identity disc. That's the name of the people who adopted her."

"Is she going to be all right, mate?" asked Chris, gently stroking her chin with one finger. Holly twisted her head and licked his glove with a tiny pink tongue.

Neil was relieved to feel her tail thud against his chest – she was obviously feeling better already. "She's just cold, scared and worn out," he said. "But she'll be fine when she's warmed up and had a rest."

Emily and Julie clambered up the hill, pulling the sledges. Jake was off the lead now and he was carrying Neil's missing glove in his mouth. He dropped it at Neil's feet, then sat down proudly, his wagging tail sweeping the loose snow from side to side.

"Well done, Jake," Neil praised. He felt in his pocket for a dog treat but the packet wasn't there.

Emily laughed. "I don't think Jake should have any more treats. He found the packet under the bush while he was searching for your glove and wolfed most of them!"

"Ben helped him as well," giggled Julie.

Neil grinned and patted the Border collie's head. Then he pulled the glove on gratefully, suddenly realizing how chilled his hand was.

"What are we going to do with her?" asked Emily, fondling Holly's ears.

Neil scanned the hillside. "Nobody seems to be looking for her so we'd better take her back to her home. Her owners live in one of those old cottages that back on to the ridgeway. I remember thinking it was an ideal place for a dog—" He broke off, frowning. Once again, he tried to imagine what sort of people would let a young puppy wander off alone in the snow. His mum and dad always checked that rescue dogs were going to good homes but perhaps they'd made a mistake this time. . .

"Have you found homes for the other Labrador puppies?" asked Julie as they trudged along the ridgeway. She stroked the top of Holly's head and Neil felt the puppy's tail wagging again inside his coat.

"No, the other three are still at the rescue centre," he said.

Julie frowned. "You'd think loads of people would want to adopt gorgeous little creatures like this."

Holly gave a tiny high-pitched bark, as

16

though she'd understood what Julie said and fully agreed.

"I'm sure we'll find homes for the others soon," said Neil. "I want to see them all settled by Christmas."

Chris whistled. "Do you reckon you'll do it? Homing three puppies in a week is pushing it a bit, isn't it, mate?"

Neil squared his shoulders determinedly. "We'll do it."

They reached the end of the ridgeway. Low-roofed, old-fashioned cottages were clearly visible through the leafless trees ahead. Neil and Emily said goodbye to Chris, Hasheem and Julie, and set off along a narrow path that led between two of the cottages to the quiet road beyond. Jake and Ben touched noses, then Jake trotted quickly after Neil.

It didn't take long to find Ridgeview Cottage, the Morgans' house. Neil marched up to the front door and rang the bell, with Emily and Jake close behind.

A plump, anxious-looking woman opened the door. "Mrs Morgan?" Emily asked politely.

The woman nodded. "That's right." Suddenly she caught sight of the puppy peeping out from inside Neil's coat and her face lit up. "Holly!

Thank goodness! We've been looking everywhere for you," she said before Neil had a chance to speak. She held out her hands and Neil placed Holly in her arms.

"It's all right, girl," he said soothingly. "You're home now."

"She is all right, isn't she?" Mrs Morgan asked, concerned.

"She seems fine – just a bit scared," Neil said. "Er. . . why exactly was she out on her own?"

"I let her out in the garden," said Mrs Morgan. "I thought it was safe. When I went to fetch her a couple of minutes later she just wasn't there. There must be a hole in the fence." She hugged the little puppy. "I've been so worried about her."

Mrs Morgan ushered Neil, Emily and Jake inside. "Thank you so much for bringing her home," she said, leading the way into a large, welcoming kitchen at the front of the house. "My husband's still out searching for her – he'll be so relieved."

A log fire was burning cheerfully at one end of the kitchen, its flickering flames casting an orange glow across the flagstone floor. Mrs Morgan crossed to a large airing cupboard and took out a pink, fluffy towel. Then she sat down in a chair, cradled Holly on her lap and rubbed her dry.

"Would you like to sit down?" Mrs Morgan asked, smiling up at Neil and Emily.

They settled down on the big, comfortable sofa, while Jake lay down by the fire. Neil relaxed. He'd been angry with the Morgans for letting Holly roam free but now it seemed that he'd made a mistake. Mrs Morgan was clearly just as concerned about the Labrador as he was.

"She's a smashing little pup," said Neil, watching the Labrador, who had curled up on Mrs Morgan's lap and was dozing contentedly.

"Yes, Holly's going to be our daughter's dog," explained Mrs Morgan. "We only moved here two weeks ago and a few days before that our dog died." She sighed. "We'd had her for sixteen years and we all miss her badly, but our daughter Alex is heartbroken."

They heard a door open at the back of the house. "I can't find her anywhere," a man's worried voice called. "I've been all over the ridgeway but—"

"It's all right, John," Mrs Morgan interrupted. "Holly's home. Some kind people have brought her back." She turned to Neil. "How did you know where to bring Holly?"

"We recognized her and then saw your name on her collar," explained Neil. "Our parents own King Street Kennels and I remember them saying that Holly's new owners lived here."

Mrs Morgan smiled. "You must be Neil, then. Alex is going to be in your class at school. And you must be Emily. Your dad told me all about you two."

A tall, smiling man came into the room. He was still wearing his coat and hat and his face was red with cold. "What a relief!" He took off his gloves and patted Holly affectionately. She lifted her head and blinked at him, then fell asleep again. "Thanks for bringing her home. Where did you find her?"

"Up on the ridgeway. We were sledging there," said Emily. "In fact, we're going back there now. Do you think Alex would like to come with us?"

"It's kind of you to ask, Emily," Mrs Morgan said. "I'm sure she'd love to, but she's not here. She's been staying at her grandparents' in Manchester since we moved so she could finish the term at her old school." She glanced at her watch. "I thought they'd have arrived by now, though," she added. "Her gran's bringing her over. Perhaps the snow's held them up."

"She doesn't know about Holly yet," explained Mr Morgan. "But she'll be really excited when she meets her." As he spoke, a red car drew up outside. "At last! Here they are," he said. "I'll go and let them in."

Neil and Emily watched through the window as Alex and her grandmother came up the snowy path, each carrying a suitcase. Alex was tall and skinny, with long dark hair pulled back into a ponytail. She wasn't wearing a coat and the falling snow speckled her black jumper. She looked just like a Dalmatian in reverse, Neil thought, grinning to himself.

Holly opened her eyes and sat up, refreshed by her nap. Mrs Morgan put her down on the floor. "Alex is coming, girl," she said.

Holly wagged her tail and gave a tiny bark. Jake stood up, obviously intending to go and make friends with the puppy, but Neil told him to stay and the Border collie sat down again obediently.

Neil heard Mr Morgan say hello to his daughter. "Go through into the kitchen, Alex," he continued. "We've got a surprise for you."

Alex appeared in the doorway, followed by her dad and her gran. "Hello, love," said Mrs

Morgan, giving her a hug. "Meet Holly. She's
your new dog."

Alex's smile faded. She stared at Holly in
horror. "How could you? I don't want a new
dog," she cried, and burst into tears.

Chapter Three

"If I can't have Daisy I don't want any dog," sobbed Alex. "Don't you understand that?"

"But Daisy's not with us any more, love," Mrs Morgan said gently. She tried to put her arms round her daughter, but Alex pulled away.

Holly trotted towards Alex, her tail wagging and her mouth open in a welcoming grin. "Look, she likes you already," Mr Morgan said encouragingly.

Alex shook her head. "I don't want her. I'm never having another dog." She stumbled out of the room with tears pouring down her cheeks. Her gran followed her, calling to her to come back.

Holly sat down suddenly and stared after Alex, whining. Neil was just about to go to her when Mrs Morgan picked her up. "It's all right, Holly," she said reassuringly, stroking the puppy who nestled against her.

Neil knew how Alex was feeling. When his own dog, Sam, had died, he'd been devastated. But at least he'd had Jake, Sam's son, to ease the pain. He bent down to stroke Jake, running his hand over the Border collie's coat and letting Jake nuzzle his neck. It was never easy when a dog died, he thought, but in the end you had to move on. There were so many other dogs in need of a loving home.

"Oh dear," said Mr Morgan, staring after Alex in dismay. "What on earth are we going to do now?"

"I really don't know." Mrs Morgan's shoulders slumped. "I was sure she'd fall in love with Holly the moment she saw her."

There was an awkward silence.

"Look," said Neil, "if you like, we could take Holly back to the rescue centre – just for the moment."

The Morgans exchanged worried glances. "Perhaps it would be best," Mr Morgan said hesitantly.

"She'll be back with her brothers and sister," Neil pointed out.

"And maybe Alex will change her mind," added Emily. "After all, how could she resist such a gorgeous little pup?"

"I hope you're right," Mr Morgan said.

Mrs Morgan shook her head firmly. "I'm sure Alex will realize she wants her soon. She's probably thinking it over right now."

"But you know how stubborn she can be sometimes," Mr Morgan reminded her.

Mrs Morgan bit her lip. "I know. But poor Holly. She's such a lovely puppy. *I* don't like the idea of having to part with her." She hugged the Labrador tightly.

"We just need to give Alex a bit of space," Mr Morgan said. He reached out for Holly, and Mrs Morgan handed her over reluctantly. "She may well decide she wants to keep her in a day or two," Mr Morgan reassured his wife, "but it'll be best if Holly's not here reminding Alex of Daisy while she's getting used to the idea of having another dog."

Mrs Morgan gave a weak smile. "I know you're right, John," she said. "But all the same . . ." She gave Holly one last stroke then turned to Neil. "I'll fetch her things." She hurried out of the room, returning a few moments later with a dog carrier, a soft blue blanket and a squeaky rubber bone.

Emily spread the blanket in the bottom of the dog carrier. "This will keep Holly warm on the way home," she said.

Neil took Holly from Mr Morgan and put her inside the carrier. "Good girl," he said as she snuggled into the blanket. He put the rubber bone beside her and shut the door, checking that the catch was fastened properly. "Don't worry. We'll take good care of her," he promised, straightening up. He called Jake to heel and picked up the dog carrier. Then he, Emily and Jake went back out into the snow.

"Thanks for all your help," Mrs Morgan called after them.

Neil and Emily waved as they set off. Emily pulled both sledges behind her while Neil carried Holly. "Poor thing," he said. "Let's hope Alex decides she wants her soon. If not, we're going to have to find homes for *four* puppies before Christmas!"

A grey Morris Minor was turning into King Street Kennels as Neil, Emily and Jake arrived home with Holly. "It's Gavin and Jet," Emily said. Gavin Thorpe was the young vicar of Compton and Jet, his black Labrador, always stayed at King Street Kennels when Gavin and his wife Susie went on holiday.

"I wonder if he'd like one of the Labrador puppies to keep Jet company," said Neil thoughtfully.

Emily shook her head. "I shouldn't think so. Susie's going to have her baby soon. I can hardly see her and Gavin wanting a baby and a puppy."

"Yeah, I suppose it would be difficult," Neil agreed.

The Morris Minor came to a stop on the snowy drive. Gavin climbed out and Jet jumped out after him. "Hello, you two. Lovely day," Gavin joked, looking wryly at the sky.

"Hello, Gavin," Neil and Emily said together.

Jet trotted towards them, tail wagging and eyes bright. "Hi, Jet," Neil said, running a hand over his smooth fur. He put the dog carrier down, opened its wire door and lifted Holly out, still wrapped in her blanket. Jet stretched up to sniff her. She peeped out of her blanket, her dark eyes wary as she looked at the newcomer.

"It's OK, Holly," said Neil, giving her a comforting stroke.

Emily crouched down to make a fuss of Jet and he licked her cheek affectionately. Then he turned his attention to Jake. The two dogs touched noses briefly, before launching into a boisterous game of chase that involved racing round and round Gavin's car and occasionally wriggling underneath it and out the other side.

"Have you come to book Jet in for a holiday?" asked Emily.

"Not this time," said the vicar. Jet ran back to him and Gavin ruffled his glossy black fur. "Actually I've come to ask your dad a huge favour."

"You'd better come in then," Neil said. He and Emily ushered Gavin round the side of the house and into the Parkers' kitchen. The house was warm and bright, and smelt deliciously of spicy mincemeat. A Christmas song was playing on the radio.

Carole was bending over the kitchen table, rolling out pastry. Sarah, Neil and Emily's five-year-old sister, was helping her, squeezing pastry scraps into Christmassy shapes. "I'm making an angel and Father Christmas and a stocking," she said proudly, holding up one of the shapes to show them. Her eyes widened as Holly poked her head out of the blanket. "A puppy!" she squealed, delighted. Dropping the pastry, she hurried across to Neil.

Carole Parker looked up. "Hello, Gavin," she said. "Come and sit down while I see what Neil's up to." She shot Neil a questioning glance.

"Thanks," said Gavin. He unbuttoned his coat and sat down, while Jet settled contentedly at his feet.

Carole pushed a strand of dark hair out of her face with the back of one floury hand, leaving a white streak across her forehead, then turned to Neil. "Where on earth have you got that puppy from?"

"It's Holly," Neil said gloomily, and he and Emily explained what had happened.

"You were right to bring her back," sighed Carole. She brushed flour off her hands then came to look at the puppy. "I wouldn't like to think of her belonging to someone who didn't want her," she added, rubbing the side of the pup's head with one finger. Holly stuck out a small, pink tongue and licked Carole's hand. "Poor Alex. I can understand why she'd feel like that. It's very hard to lose a dog you love. But perhaps she'll come round."

"I hope so," said Neil. He was sure Holly was just what Alex needed.

"We could keep Holly," Sarah said eagerly, stretching up on tiptoe to stroke the puppy. "She gets on really well with Jake and—"

"We are not having another dog," Carole said firmly.

"But she's really sweet—" wailed Sarah.

"No!" said Carole.

"Do you want us to put her back in the rescue centre?" asked Neil. He wished they could keep Holly but he knew it would be pointless to try to talk his mother round.

"Yes, please," Carole said. As she turned to Gavin, Jake trotted across to her and rubbed against her leg, soaking her jeans. "Jake!" she groaned.

"Yeah, he's pretty wet from being out in the snow," said Neil. "Could you give him a rub down, please? And can you make sure his feet are dry."

Carole laughed. "I do know how to look after dogs, Neil."

Neil laughed too. "Sorry."

In spite of the snow outside, the rescue centre felt deliciously warm when Neil and Emily went in. "I'll prepare a bowl of food for her," said Emily. "She must be starving after being out in the cold for so long."

"Good idea," Neil said. He fetched a towel and gently rubbed Holly's head – the only part of her that had been exposed to the weather when she'd been out of the dog carrier. By the time she was dry, her fur was standing up in chocolate-brown spikes. Neil smoothed it down, then set the puppy beside the bowl of food that Emily had prepared. She tucked in hungrily.

When she'd finished eating, Neil carried her to the pen that her sister and brothers shared. The pups were in their basket, lying asleep in a contented heap. Holly whined and wagged her tail as she picked up their scent. The puppies stirred.

"Come on, you lazy lot. Wake up and say hello to your sister," Neil called as Emily unfastened the door. The smallest puppy, a black Labrador who they had named Santa, struggled out from underneath his heavier golden sister, Candy, and darted to the wire. He eyed Holly inquisitively, his tail swinging from side to side.

Neil carried Holly into the pen and set her down. In seconds the other three puppies, two black and one golden, were all around her, sniffing her, touching noses and welcoming her home. Then the four of them plunged into a wild and joyful game of chase.

Neil watched with mixed emotions. It was good that the puppies were pleased to see Holly but he couldn't help feeling sorry for her. The rescue centre was warm and comfortable but it wasn't nearly as nice as the Morgans' house. She'd miss the attention that the Morgans had given her too, Neil thought. He made up his mind to visit her as often as he could.

Gavin, Carole and Bob were chatting and drinking coffee when Neil and Emily went indoors. Jake and Jet were lying by the stove.

Jake sprang up and trotted across to Neil, leaping up to lick his face.

"Down, boy," Neil commanded.

Jake sat down obediently, watching Neil intently, his bright eyes sparkling.

"You've got him well trained," said Gavin admiringly.

Neil laughed. "Most of the time. But he has his moments, don't you, Jake?" The Border collie barked in response.

"Anyway, Gavin, can we do something for you, or is this just a social visit?" Bob asked.

"I'm after some help, I'm afraid," said the vicar.

Bob stroked his beard thoughtfully. "I'll help out if I can, but we're a bit pushed for time today. Bev and Kate aren't working and this snow means that simple jobs take twice as long." Bev and Kate were King Street Kennels' hard-working and committed kennel maids.

Gavin nodded. "The snow's caused problems on the roads, too. I hope it's not going to take me too long to get home – I don't like leaving Susie on her own." He produced a mobile phone from his pocket and checked that it was switched on. "She's going to ring me if anything happens. The baby's due in ten days' time."

Carole smiled. "You must be really excited."

"I can't wait," Gavin said. "Our first son or daughter!"

"So do you want me to drive you both to the hospital in the Range Rover when the time comes?" asked Bob.

Gavin shook his head. "It's not that. It's rather an unusual favour actually." Neil thought he looked slightly embarrassed. "You see, I'm going to set up a Christmas grotto in the church hall – for children and dogs."

"That sounds ace!" Neil cried.

Bob laughed. "A Christmas grotto for dogs?" He put down his empty coffee mug. "It's an original idea – I'll give you that."

"We've got to raise some money to get the church hall roof repaired," said Gavin. "There are so many dogs in Compton I thought that people might be willing to pay a small amount to bring their kids *and* their dogs to see Father Christmas."

"I'll bring Jake," said Neil. "He'll love seeing all his doggy friends." He ruffled the Border collie's ears and Jake's tail thumped rhythmically on the floor. "Loads of people will come. Doctor Harvey will bring Finn and Sandy—" Neil began.

"And Julie and Ben will come," Emily chipped in. "And Steve and Ricky."

"I bet Mrs Jepson will bring Sugar and Spice," said Neil, with a laugh. "In fact, she'll probably bring them four times at least." Sugar and Spice were the most pampered pooches in Compton.

"So where does Bob come into this?" asked Carole.

Gavin blushed slightly and twisted his empty coffee mug round and round. "I was hoping you'd dress up as Father Christmas, Bob," he mumbled.

Neil, Emily and Carole all laughed.

"Father Christmas! Me?" Bob shook his head. "You are joking?"

"No. You'd be perfect. You've got a real way with dogs," the vicar insisted.

"Well maybe. . . But what about the kids?" asked Bob.

Gavin smiled. "Oh I'm sure they'll be as good as gold. Will you do it?"

"I don't know . . ." Bob began, pulling a face.

"Oh go on, Dad," cried Emily. "You'd be brilliant."

"You'd look great in that red suit," Neil chuckled. "You might have to dye your beard, though."

Sarah came into the kitchen, carrying her hamster, Fudge, in her cupped hands. She was frowning. "Shhh," she said crossly. "I'm trying to teach Fudge to dance. He wants to be a ballerina, like me." Sarah thought her hamster was the cleverest creature in the world.

Neil started to laugh, then hastily changed it into a cough as Sarah turned a furious face towards him. "How's he getting on, Squirt?" he asked.

"He was doing really well until you all started laughing and putting him off," huffed Sarah.

"What's so funny, anyway?"

"Dad's going to dress up as Father Christmas and give out presents to dogs and children," Emily explained.

"Why can't the real Father Christmas do it?" asked Sarah.

"He's too busy," said Gavin. "But he's quite happy for your dad to stand in for him." The vicar turned to Bob. "So will you do it?"

"Of course he will," Carole said quickly. "And he'll enjoy every minute of it."

"There's your answer, then," said Bob with a grin. "If Carole says I'll do it, then I'll do it."

"Excellent." Gavin beamed at him. "I've got a big sack of presents in the boot of my car. I was wondering whether you and Emily might be able to wrap them for me, Neil?"

"We'd love to," Emily said eagerly.

"I'll give you a hand bringing them in," offered Neil.

The vicar stood up. "Thanks for the coffee, Carole. And thanks for agreeing to stand in for Father Christmas, Bob," he said with a wink. He called to Jet and the black Labrador stood up and stretched.

"Let us know as soon as there's any news about the baby," said Carole.

"I will. See you soon."

The vicar followed Neil outside. It was still snowing; large white flakes curled thickly down from the heavy grey sky. The tracks that Neil and Emily had left when they had come in from the rescue centre were already half filled with snow. Neil tilted his head back so that the snow settled on his face. A few flakes drifted into his open mouth and he let them melt on his tongue.

While Gavin unlocked the boot of his Morris Minor, Neil watched Jake and Jet. The two dogs slid along the ground on their tummies, pushing the snow into heaps with their noses and front paws. Then they rolled over, barking excitedly, and leapt up again, sending the snow flying up in wild flurries.

Neil groaned. "Typical! Now Jake will have to be dried again."

Gavin lifted a black bin bag out of his boot. "Here you are, Neil. Thanks for agreeing to wrap them." He opened the car door and Jet darted across to him and jumped inside. The Labrador scrambled over the front seats and flopped down on a rug in the back. "Bye, Neil," Gavin called as he started the engine. "Good luck with those pups. I hope you manage to find homes for all of them."

"Thanks! I'm sure we will," Neil said cheerfully. But he didn't feel quite so sure. If they were going to find homes for Holly and her brothers and sister before Christmas, they'd need all the luck they could get.

Chapter Four

"I wish Gavin had bought presents that were easier to wrap," Emily said, pulling a rubber bone out of the plastic sack on the floor. "Some of these things are really fiddly."

"If you think that's difficult, have a go at one of these," said Neil, waving a pyramid-shaped puzzle at her and making the balls inside it rattle. They were sitting at the kitchen table, wrapping presents for the Christmas grotto. Jake lay stretched out on his side in front of the stove, basking in the heat.

"Hey, why don't we phone Jake Fielding about the puppies?" Emily suggested suddenly. Jake was the young reporter for the *Compton*

News and he'd helped the Parkers out before, when they'd needed publicity for their rescue dogs. "That article he did about them in the paper when they were first found was brilliant. I'm sure he'd do another one about them needing homes – and take their pictures. I bet loads of people would want to adopt them, then."

"Brilliant, Em!" said Neil. "Let's ring him straight away. And we could make posters and put them up around Compton."

"Yes. We should put an ad on the King Street Kennels' website too."

Neil finished wrapping the pyramid puzzle then fetched the bin bag and held it open by the edge of the table. "Slide the wrapped presents in here, then we'll ask Mum if we can use the office computer," he said to Emily.

They hurried to the office and found Carole hard at work on the computer.

"Oh, we were going to make some posters advertising the puppies," Neil explained, looking disappointed. "I suppose we can come back later if you're busy."

Carole shook her head and sighed. "I've had enough of office work for the moment – I'm exhausted now. The computer's all yours."

It didn't take long to make the posters. "They're nice and bright," Emily said approvingly as she took the first one out of the printer. She read it out: "*Wanted: good homes for gorgeous Labrador puppies. Apply to King Street Kennels, Compton.*" Underneath this heading was a photo of the puppies that they'd scanned into the computer. Neil had taken it the day before the puppies had moved from the Parkers' kitchen to the rescue centre. They were all sitting on the rug, gazing at the camera appealingly.

Neil phoned Jake Fielding while the posters were printing, and the reporter promised to come over the next day to take the puppies' photo. He said he could probably get the story in that week's issue of the *Compton News*.

"Loads of people will see them in the paper," said Emily, when Neil had rung off and told her the good news. "I bet we'll get hundreds of people phoning about them."

Neil laughed. "We don't need hundreds. Only three. . . Or four," he added, "if Alex doesn't come back for Holly."

"Do you think she will come?" Emily asked.

Neil shrugged. "I hope so. Anyway, let's not worry about Alex now. We need to update the

King Street Kennels website." He connected to the Internet, then added the puppies' details and their photo to the website. "There," he said. "I just hope lots of people read it."

Neil and Emily put the posters into a plastic bag to keep them dry, then set off for Compton with Jake. It had stopped snowing but there was no sign of a thaw. They walked quickly, their footsteps muffled by the deep snow that covered the pavement. "I hope this weather lasts," said Neil as they turned into the high street. "A white Christmas would be ace!"

Strings of coloured lights hung across the high street and most of the shops had a decorated tree in the window.

They reached the supermarket and Emily took a poster inside. When she came out again an assistant was already positioning it in the window. "Wow! It looks brilliant!" Neil whooped. "People will spot it from a mile off."

"No one will be able to resist having a puppy when they see that photo," said Emily.

They continued down the high street, taking posters into the greengrocer's and the shoe shop. Neil glanced back at them as he walked towards the baker's. "There are already people looking— Oof!" he gasped suddenly as he collided with someone and stumbled backwards.

Jake darted over and jumped up at him. He seemed to think Neil was playing a game. "Get off, you daft dog," Neil said. He gently pushed Jake down, and saw Alex standing beside him, holding a loaf of bread and grinning.

"Are you all right?" she asked.

"Fine. Was it you I bumped into?"

"Yes. But it's OK. You've only dented my loaf a bit," Alex laughed, bending down to stroke Jake. "Your dog's lovely," she said, rubbing his head. "What's his name?"

"This is Jake," Emily said.

Neil watched her making a fuss of the young Border collie. It was obvious that she loved dogs and he wished that he could persuade her to take Holly. The two of them would be good for each other.

"We've made some posters advertising the puppies," said Neil. "Do you want to give us a hand with them? We're trying to persuade shopkeepers to display them." Perhaps helping to find homes for the puppies would make Alex realize that she did want Holly after all, he thought.

Alex looked doubtful. "I don't think . . ." she began hesitantly.

"Oh go on," Neil pleaded, holding out a poster to her. "We could really do with some help, couldn't we, Em?"

Emily looked puzzled but she nodded anyway.

"All right, then." Alex took a poster. "Aren't they gorgeous?" she said, looking at their picture. "I should think everyone will—" She broke off and bit her lip, but Neil felt certain she'd been about to say that everyone would want to adopt one.

As soon as Alex took the poster into the baker's shop, Emily turned to Neil.

"Why were you so desperate for Alex to help?" she asked. "I mean, it's not as if we can't manage."

"I thought she'd be more likely to take Holly if she was involved in finding homes for the other puppies," he explained.

"Ah. . . nice idea," Emily said approvingly.

Alex reappeared a moment later, smiling broadly. "They're going to put it up."

"Brilliant!" said Neil. He handed Alex another poster. "Do you want to try the sweet shop next?"

They carried on through the centre of Compton until they had run out of posters.

"My grandad used to breed Shelties," Alex said as they turned to walk home. "He goes to loads of doggy events. If you print out some more posters I'll ask him to put them up in Manchester – if you like."

"That would be ace!" Emily said enthusiastically. "The more people who hear about the puppies, the more chance we've got of finding homes for all of them."

Alex looked wistful for a moment. "Are they all good-natured?" she asked.

"Oh, yes," Emily said. "They've all got their own personalities. Santa's very sweet – he's the little black one. Candy, the golden one, is inquisitive, Cracker's really playful but Holly's the most friendly."

"Why don't you come and visit Holly at the rescue centre?" Neil suggested. "I'm sure she'd be glad to see you. And you could meet her brothers and sister too."

Alex shook her head unhappily. "No, thanks."

"I expect Holly will be feeling a bit lonely at the moment," Neil went on. "She lived with your mum and dad for four days so she's used to having people around her. She could definitely use some company." He didn't tell her that he was constantly popping into the rescue centre with Emily and Sarah to see the puppies. After spending so many weeks hand-rearing them in their kitchen, they all wanted to see as much of them as possible.

Alex shook her head again, more firmly this time. Her eyes were sad. "*Daisy* was my dog. I don't want another one." There was an awkward silence. Neil realized that persuading Alex to take Holly back wasn't going to be an easy task.

"Why don't you help us with the Christmas grotto at the church, then?" asked Emily, changing the subject. "We promised the vicar we'd wrap all the presents. We've made a start but there's loads more to do."

Alex frowned.

"Oh, go on," Neil said. "We'll never get them done on our own." *Perhaps we'll be able to persuade Alex to visit Holly once she is at King Street*, he thought hopefully.

Alex nodded. "All right," she agreed, looking a bit less miserable.

"Come round tomorrow morning," said Emily. "And—" She broke off suddenly as somebody called her name.

A blond boy was dashing towards them, weaving in and out of the shoppers on the pavement. "Emily! Hey, Emily!"

"It's Tom Charlton," Emily said. "He's in my class at school."

Tom pounded up to them, his face glowing with excitement, and skidded to a halt. "I saw your posters!" he panted. "I've just moved to a house with a garden and my mum and dad said I could have a dog. Will you save one of your puppies for me?"

"It's not quite as simple as that," Neil explained. "My parents will want to talk to your mum or dad before they let you have one of the puppies. But I'm sure it will be OK," he added quickly as he saw Tom's face fall. "When do you want to come?"

"How about tomorrow morning?" asked Tom eagerly.

"OK, come over at about half past ten," Neil said.

"You won't let them all go before then, will you?" Tom asked.

"No, of course not," Neil promised.

"I don't know which one I'll choose. They're all gorgeous," Tom said.

"They certainly are," Emily agreed.

"See you tomorrow then," said Tom. He raced away.

"Our poster campaign's working!" Emily cried, delighted. "At this rate *all* the puppies will be gone by Christmas."

Neil turned to speak to Alex but she wasn't there. "Hey, where's Alex gone?" he asked. He looked along the high street and saw her hurrying away with her head down. Neil guessed she was thinking about Daisy. But perhaps she was feeling guilty too, for rejecting Holly when Tom was obviously so enthusiastic about giving one of the pups a home. Or perhaps she was even worried that Tom might choose Holly.

"Poor Alex," said Emily. "She looks so unhappy."

"Holly would know how to cheer her up," said Neil. "We've just got to find a way of making her see it . . ."

Chapter Five

"The phone!" Neil cried, jumping up from the breakfast table next morning. "Perhaps it's somebody ringing about the puppies!"

Bob Parker laid a restraining hand on his arm. "I don't want you scaring a potential customer away by begging them to take one of the pups," he laughed, and went out of the room to answer it himself.

Neil sat down again. Jake, who was sitting beside him, watched hopefully as he bit into a slice of toast. "You've had your breakfast, Jake," Neil laughed.

The Border collie gave him a doggy grin and thumped the floor with his tail.

"That was Gavin, calling from the hospital," said Bob, reappearing in the kitchen doorway. "The baby's on the way now – over a week early. Poor Gavin's worried about the grotto, and he's asked if we could start decorating it later."

"Brilliant!" Emily cried.

"You bet!" whooped Neil.

"What about you, Sarah?" Carole asked. "Do you want to help decorate the Christmas grotto?"

Sarah shook her head. "No. I'm giving Fudge a dancing lesson. And I'm making a Christmas card for the puppies."

Bob drained his mug of tea. "That hamster must be the best dancer in the world." As he headed for the back door there was a knock on the front door. Emily hurried to answer it and came back with Alex.

"Oh I'm sorry," said Alex, looking at the breakfast table. "Have I come too early?"

"Of course not," Neil said, reaching for another slice of toast.

"Neil," Carole laughed. "Haven't you had enough yet?"

Neil shook his head. "Nearly. This is Alex, Mum. She's going to help us wrap the presents for the grotto."

"Hello, Alex. Would you like some breakfast?" Carole asked.

"No thanks," said Alex. "I've only just had mine."

"Nobody's phoned about the puppies yet," Neil said, while he and Emily cleared the kitchen table. "I visited them this morning. Holly seemed a bit miserable but she perked up when she saw me." He watched Alex as he spoke. She definitely looked interested when he mentioned Holly, and Neil was convinced that was a good sign.

They sat round the kitchen table and set to work wrapping presents. Jake watched them curiously for a while, then he flopped down by the stove for a nap.

"Perhaps you and I could take the money at the grotto, Alex," suggested Emily.

Alex smiled. "That'd be great! I might get to meet some people then. It's funny living in Compton and not knowing anyone. I had loads of friends in Manchester."

"I'll introduce you to some of my friends from school, if you like," said Neil. "You're going to be in my class so you'll get to know them soon anyway."

"I'd like that," Alex said, cutting off a length

of sticky tape. "By the way, I phoned my grandad last night and told him about the puppies. He said I could send him some posters – and he's going to ring his friends to see if they know anyone who wants a puppy."

"Ace!" Neil finished wrapping a squeaky dog ball and put the parcel on the growing pile in the centre of the table. "I'll print out some posters for you today."

Just then Neil heard the sound of a car turning into the drive. He looked out of the window to see who it was. "It's Tom and his dad," he told Emily and Alex. "They're bang on time – Tom really must be keen!"

As soon as Neil opened the door, Tom asked anxiously, "You have kept me a puppy, haven't you?"

Neil grinned. "Yes, don't worry." It was good to see somebody so genuinely enthusiastic about adopting a dog. Neil was already sure that Tom would make a good owner.

Tom's eyes lit up. "Brilliant," he said, following Neil across the yard to the rescue centre. "I've wanted a dog for ages and ages." He grinned at his dad, a friendly-looking man with short ginger hair. "Now I'm going to get one at last."

"Wait for us," Emily called as she and Alex came out of the house. "We're coming too!" Emily dashed after them, but Neil saw that Alex followed more slowly.

"How did you persuade her to come?" Neil whispered, when Emily caught up with him.

"I said I needed her to help me feed them." Emily grinned.

"Nice one!" said Neil.

Bob came out of Kennel Block One and shook hands with Mr Charlton. "You're interested in one of our Labrador pups, I hear," he said warmly.

"That's right," confirmed Mr Charlton.

"Come into the office and we'll discuss the details while Tom's choosing the puppy he thinks he'd like. Could you take Tom into the rescue centre, Neil?"

"Right." Neil led the way inside. Holly and Candy trotted up to the wire netting of their pen and watched as Neil, Emily and Tom approached. Santa and Cracker, the two black puppies, were curled up in their basket, side by side. Cracker opened an eye sleepily, then lumbered to his feet. Santa yawned lazily as he stood up and stretched.

"They're gorgeous!" Tom cried. He crouched down and pushed his fingers through the wire. The puppies crowded round, their tails wagging with excitement. Alex watched from a distance, her face tense and pale.

"There are two girls and two boys," said Neil. He opened the door of the pen and went inside, followed by Emily and Tom. Alex hung back at first, but Emily eventually persuaded her to come in. To Neil's delight, Holly rushed straight over to Alex, barking a greeting.

"She remembers you!" Emily said.

Alex nodded, frowning. She tried not to look at the puppy but Holly was clearly determined to be noticed. She scrambled on to Alex's foot and pawed at her leg, whining.

"Do you want to hold her?" asked Neil.

Alex shook her head, but she crouched down and rumpled Holly's silky ears. The puppy licked the inside of Alex's wrist, her tail lashing from side to side. Alex leant forward and spoke softly to Holly. Neil couldn't hear what she was saying but he was pleased to see that Alex's frown had faded.

The other three puppies wouldn't leave Tom alone. They banged each other aside in their determination to get his full attention. Eventually he sat down and let them clamber on to his lap. "They're fantastic!" he said, beaming at Neil and Emily. "They're just fantastic!"

He picked up Santa and held him against his chest. "But this one's the best of all. Look at his cute little face." The puppy nuzzled Tom's neck, then stretched up and licked his ear.

Tom laughed. "Hey, that tickles! I'd like this one, please. What's his name?"

"Santa," Emily said.

"That's perfect," said Tom.

Emily picked up the other two puppies, so Tom and Santa could get to know each other properly. Holly had pressed herself against

Alex's ankle and fallen asleep. Alex was still stroking her. Neil felt frustrated. He wouldn't dream of trying to get Alex to take Holly if he thought she couldn't cope with her, but it was clear that a bond was growing between the two of them.

The outer door of the rescue centre opened and Bob and Mr Charlton came in. "All the paperwork's done," Bob announced. "It looks like you and your family will make very good dog owners, Tom."

Tom grinned and stood up, holding Santa carefully. "I've chosen this one, Dad. He's called Santa. Can we take him home now?"

"I'll fetch the dog carrier from the car," Mr Charlton laughed.

Santa was soon safely inside the carrier and Tom headed eagerly for the door, obviously impatient to show Santa his new home.

"Thanks very much," Mr Charlton said, shaking hands with Bob.

"Happy Christmas!" Tom called as he followed his dad out into the snow, holding the carrier carefully.

When Tom and Santa had gone, Emily and Alex fed the remaining puppies.

Neil fetched a ball and threw it across the

pen. The three puppies dashed after it, barking eagerly. Then they raced round and round their pen, chasing the ball, each other and their own tails until at last they flopped down, worn out from so much exercise. Once again, Holly chose to settle down beside Alex, with her head and front paws on Alex's foot.

"She's really fond of you," Neil pointed out.

Alex looked down sadly at the tiny puppy. "She's lovely," she said, "but I just don't want another dog. It's no use trying to persuade me."

"I felt like that when my dog Sam died," Neil began. He thought back to that terrible day when Sam's weak heart had finally failed after he'd rescued Jake from drowning. "But—"

"Look, Emily told me about that," Alex interrupted. "And I'm sorry about Sam. But it's not the same. You already had Jake. I didn't have another dog . . ." She broke off, obviously trying to make sense of her feelings. "It wouldn't be fair to Daisy," she said at last. Her eyes filled with tears and she brushed them away. "She was the best dog ever."

Emily put her arm round her. "Daisy wouldn't—"

She didn't get a chance to finish because the door of the rescue centre opened and Jake

Fielding came in. He was a tall young man who wore his long hair in a ponytail. He had a camera slung round his neck and a tripod under his arm. "Your dad said I'd find you in here," he said. "I've come to take some pictures of these pups of yours for the paper."

"Hi, Jake," said Neil. "Thanks for coming." He grinned at him, but inside he was feeling even more frustrated. What a shame Jake had arrived at that moment! Neil was pretty sure that he and Emily could have convinced Alex to take Holly if they hadn't been interrupted.

"Can you each hold one of the puppies, please?" Jake said as Neil let him into the pen. He quickly set up his tripod and attached his camera to the top.

Emily picked up Holly and plonked her in Alex's arms. Then she scooped up Candy, leaving Neil to hold Cracker.

"Cor, we must be overfeeding you," joked Neil as he picked him up. "You weigh a ton." The puppy nudged Neil with his nose, then stared at the camera.

"Move in closer together," Jake said, bending over to look through the camera's viewfinder. There was a flash as he took the picture.

Holly whimpered. "It's all right, girl," Alex

said soothingly.

"I'll just take a couple more," said Jake. His camera flashed again. "Our readers will be pleased to see how well they're looking." He took a final photo then put his camera back in its case and folded up his tripod. "Thanks very much, you lot. They'll be in this week's paper."

"Let's hope it does the trick," Neil said as he placed Cracker in the basket.

He watched Alex put Holly down beside her brother. She stroked Holly's head gently. The chocolate-brown Labrador rolled over and Alex tickled her tummy.

Neil looked at Emily and they both shook their heads. When was Alex going to realize that she and Holly were made for each other?

Chapter Six

"Jet's so well trained," said Neil admiringly as Bob parked the Range Rover outside the church later that afternoon. He watched the vicar's black Labrador nose around the snowy headstones. "He never goes out of the churchyard, you know, even when the gate's open."

"Does he live here, then?" Alex asked in surprise.

"He's the vicar's dog," Neil explained. "He's got his own dog flap so he can come and go as he pleases." He pointed to the back door of the vicarage, which was just visible through the trees on the far side of the churchyard.

Bob opened the car door. "Come on, you lot!

No slacking! There's work to be done."

Jake tried to scramble over into the front seat but Neil held him back. "Not that way, Jake," he laughed. "Wait your turn!" He climbed out and Jake dashed after him. Emily and Alex followed with the bag of presents.

As they went into the churchyard, Jet came bounding over. Jake sniffed Jet, then sprang away from him and disappeared behind an old weather-beaten gravestone, barking playfully. Jet stared after him for a moment, as though he was trying to decide whether to play or not. He soon made up his mind, and bounded after the younger dog.

Neil, Emily and Alex watched the two dogs darting in and out of a row of yew trees in a boisterous game of tag. "Jake seems to have cheered Jet up!" Emily laughed. She picked up the bag of presents. "Let's get started on this grotto."

"I'll have to leave you to it, I'm afraid," said Bob. "I've got to get some shopping but I'll be back later."

"Last minute Christmas presents, by any chance?" Neil said curiously.

Bob grinned. "Never you mind. You just go and get cracking on that grotto." He went out of the churchyard, shutting the gate behind him.

Neil led the way through the heavy door of the church porch, which Gavin always kept unlocked in the daytime. From there they went through a side door into the stone church hall, which was hundreds of years old, but felt light and airy inside.

Emily put the sack of presents down by the door, making sure that it was left ajar so that Jake could get in and out. They found a stepladder and an artificial Christmas tree leaning against a wall. In the middle of the polished wooden floor was a carved chair, a fold-up screen and a stack of cardboard boxes filled with Christmas decorations.

"It looks like Gavin's got all the gear together," said Neil. "If we set the screen up over here, Dad can sit behind it." He carried it to the end of the room and opened it out. "People can go in at one end, have a chat with Dad and collect their present, then come out at the other end."

"I'm going to start decorating the Christmas tree," Emily said. "It'll look nice in front of that screen."

"I'll give you a hand," Alex offered eagerly. She rummaged through one of the boxes and pulled out lengths of gold and silver foil. "Hey! These will look great fixed to the screen, Neil. We just need some drawing pins. . ."

By the time Jake came trotting in from the churchyard, the screen and ceiling were draped with glittering foil and the Christmas tree was transformed into a magical creation of glowing lights, gleaming baubles and shimmering tinsel. Neil thought it looked fantastic.

The Border collie stopped in the doorway and stared curiously. The Christmas tree lights were reflected in his dark eyes. "What do you think then, Jake?" Emily asked, stroking him.

Jake barked once, as though he approved of what he saw, then he pushed past Emily and thrust his head inquisitively into one of the cardboard boxes. When he emerged, strands of silver foil hung from his ears.

Neil laughed. "He didn't want to be outdone by a Christmas tree, did you, Jake?" he said from the stepladder where he was fixing a star to the top of the tree.

"I think he looks sweet," chuckled Alex.

Jake turned his attention to another box. It had higher sides than the first box and he couldn't see into it. Suddenly he jumped up and rested his front paws on the edge of the box.

"Don't do that!" Neil cried. His warning came too late – the box toppled over, spilling its contents over the startled dog.

Jake jumped back. A string of fairy lights was draped across his back now, and scattered around him there were baubles, silver bells and plastic reindeers and snowmen.

"Here, Jake," Neil called, climbing down from the ladder. Jake trotted across to him, trailing the lights. Laughing, Neil lifted the light cable off the young dog's back and brushed the foil strands from his ears.

"I wonder where Jet's got to," said Emily.

"I hope he's gone back into the vicarage," Neil said. "If Jake can cause this much mayhem on his own, imagine what two dogs could get up to!"

Alex stood the box upright and began to pile the decorations into it. "We could hang these snowmen and reindeer from the coat hooks," she suggested. "And the lights could go round the door."

"Good idea," Emily said, picking up two of the snowmen and hanging them on hooks. She stood back to admire the effect.

"There's a socket behind the door," Neil said, "so we'll be able to plug in the lights."

Suddenly they heard footsteps in the church porch and Jake darted out of the hall. "How are you getting on?" Bob called.

"Come and see, Dad," said Emily.

"Fantastic," Bob said enthusiastically as he looked around. "Have you put the presents behind that screen?"

"No, they're still in the porch," said Emily. "I left them by the door because I thought they'd get in the way while we were decorating."

"But you've brought some of them in here?" Bob persisted.

Neil shook his head. "No. We'll bring them in now. We're going to arrange them around your chair."

Bob looked concerned.

"What's wrong?" Neil asked anxiously.

"Come and see," said Bob grimly, ushering them out of the hall.

The sack containing the presents was still beside the door where Emily had left it. But as he drew near, Neil could see that it was half empty. "Hey, what's happened? Where have all the presents gone?"

"I suppose someone must have taken them," Bob said, puzzled.

"You mean, stolen them!" said Neil angrily.

"The thief must have come into the porch while we were working on the grotto," Emily said miserably. "We wouldn't have heard the door because I left it open for Jake – and we were all talking anyway."

"But who'd steal Christmas presents from a church?" asked Alex. "That's a horrible thing to do."

"The presents might not have been stolen," Bob said in a calm voice. "You mustn't jump to conclusions."

Neil looked round. "You don't think the thief is still here, do you?"

"He would have run off when he heard Dad

coming," Emily said. "But maybe we can find his footprints in the snow and see which way he's gone."

"It's worth a try," said Neil. He whistled for Jake and went outside, with Emily and Alex close behind him.

But the path through the churchyard had been well trampled. There were several sets of footprints on it and trying to distinguish one set from another was an impossible task.

"What I don't understand is why the thief only took some of the presents?" Alex said thoughtfully. "If he heard your dad coming, surely he could have picked up the whole sack and run off with it."

Neil nodded. Alex was right. "Maybe he's planning to come back for the rest of the presents when we've gone home," he said. "He could be hiding somewhere nearby, keeping an eye on us."

Neil scanned the churchyard and started to make his way towards the road to see if he could spot anyone suspicious-looking there. Suddenly he heard a cough behind him. He whirled round, heart thudding. Gavin was walking towards him. "Sorry, Neil," he said. "I didn't mean to startle you. How are you getting on with the grotto?"

Neil told the vicar about the missing presents. Gavin shook his head, perplexed. "It must be a misunderstanding. I'm sure nobody would steal little presents like that."

When Neil had checked the road, they headed back to the church hall, lost in thought.

"Has Neil told you about the missing presents?" Emily asked.

Gavin nodded. "But I'm sure there's a perfectly innocent explanation. Let's have a look at Santa's grotto," he said cheerfully.

Neil led the way back to the hall.

"Oh, you've done a wonderful job," the vicar said, clearly impressed.

"It's all been a waste of time, though," Neil said glumly. "The grotto will have to be cancelled if there aren't enough presents for Father Christmas to give out."

"I'll get some more," Gavin said. "People have been looking forward to this, and I can't cancel it now."

"But you won't make any money for the roof repairs if you have to buy more presents," said Emily.

"I'll be happy to supply dog treats, Gavin," Bob offered.

"Thanks, Bob. That's kind of you. That means I only need to buy presents for the children." Gavin smiled at Emily. "Don't look so worried. We'll still make a little bit of profit, it just won't be as much as I'd hoped."

"I think we should hide the rest of the presents," said Neil, "just in case the thief comes back."

"We could tuck some into the Christmas tree," Alex suggested. "If we push them in far enough, they'll be hidden in the branches."

"Good idea. And if we leave the hall door open, we can put some parcels behind it." Neil scooped up an armful of presents and positioned them behind the door. Then he pushed the door back against the wall to hide the parcels, while Emily stuffed the remainder under the cushion on Father Christmas's chair.

"I've got some good news," Gavin said, when they'd finished.

"Oh, we forgot!" said Emily. "Has Susie had the baby?"

Gavin beamed round at them. "A boy. Joshua."

"Congratulations, Gavin," Bob cried, slapping him on the back.

"Thanks." Gavin looked at his watch. "I must

get a move on. I only popped home to feed Jet and take him for a walk. I want to get back to the hospital as soon as I can."

"We could feed Jet for you, if you like," suggested Neil. "And then we could take him for a long run."

Gavin's smile broadened. "That would be wonderful, Neil. Thanks." He handed Neil his back door key. "I've got a key to the front door, so post this one through the letterbox after you've locked up." He hurried away.

"I ought to go too," Alex said. "My parents will be wondering where I've got to."

"Right, I'll give you a lift, Alex," said Bob. "You two can walk back after you've seen to Jet."

"OK," Neil agreed. He whistled for Jake, and he and Emily wound their way round the gravestones to Gavin's back door.

"I wonder who did steal the presents," Emily said. "They can't be worth very much."

"Whoever it is will get a shock when he unwraps them," Neil said, with a chuckle. "Imagine his face when he finds out he's stolen a load of rubber bones and dog biscuits!"

Chapter Seven

Alex was on the doorstep of King Street Kennels just after nine o'clock the next morning. "I hope you don't mind . . . I wanted to see the puppies."

Neil was overjoyed. Perhaps, at last, she was ready to admit that she wanted Holly. Not that she looked particularly happy, he thought as he led the way through the house to the back door.

"I want to say goodbye to them," explained Alex sadly. "I expect they'll all be gone soon and my mum said I'd be upset if I hadn't seen Holly for one last time . . . She's probably right."

Neil felt a rush of sympathy for Alex as he pulled on his coat and boots. "Come on then," he said gently, leading the way across the snowy yard.

The puppies were lying in a contented heap in their basket, fast asleep, when Neil and Alex went into the rescue centre. "They're so sweet," Alex said wistfully, watching them through the wire netting.

At the sound of Alex's voice, Holly opened her eyes. She jumped out of the basket and raced across to the wire. "She's pleased to see you," said Neil. He paused, then added, "She does seem to respond to you more than to anyone else, you know." Just seeing the two of them together made Neil feel hopeful again. If anyone could persuade Alex to take Holly, it was the pup herself.

Holly pressed against the wire, whining a greeting. Alex pushed her fingers through and stroked Holly's silky chest. The Labrador pup licked her hand, then tried to scramble up the inside of the wire towards Alex's face, her tail wagging vigorously.

Neil let Alex into the pen, then started to prepare the puppies' food. Alex sat on the floor with Holly curled up in her lap. She was stroking the pup's chocolate-brown fur while Holly gazed up at her.

Neil took the food into the pen and Cracker and Candy woke up. They leapt joyfully out of their basket and raced across to the bowl, yapping with excitement. Holly stood up on Alex's lap. She hesitated for a moment, watching Alex intently. "Go and get your breakfast, girl," Alex said, giving her a gentle push.

Holly jumped down and ran to the bowl, nudging her way in between her brother and sister.

"They're great, aren't they?" said Neil.

Alex smiled. "Especially Holly. She seems so

friendly and intelligent. I bet she'd be really easy to train and—" She broke off and a look of dismay flashed across her face.

Neil groaned inwardly. One moment he was sure Alex would take Holly, the next he was sure she wouldn't. "Having another dog wouldn't make you forget Daisy," he said at last.

Alex stood up. "No," she said firmly. "I don't want another dog. It would be . . . disloyal." She headed for the door of the pen but before she reached it, the outer door of the rescue centre opened and Bob showed a middle-aged couple in. "Ah, Neil. There you are," he said. "Mr and Mrs Grant have come to choose a puppy. They'd like a female one."

Alex froze. Then she turned and looked back at Holly, her face stiff with anxiety.

"Aren't they adorable?" said Mrs Grant.

Neil let them into the pen and Mrs Grant bent down and called to the puppies. They looked up from their bowl, hesitated, then continued to eat. "They'll probably come to you as soon as they've finished eating," Neil told the Grants. "The golden one and the brown one are both girls."

He turned to Alex. "Look, why don't you take

Holly?" he whispered urgently. "If you don't, someone else will pick her."

"I don't want her." Alex spoke fiercely but her eyes were sad.

"The brown one's gorgeous," said Mr Grant as Holly trotted away from the bowl. He picked her up. "She looks sturdy and intelligent."

Mrs Grant picked up Candy. "This one's lovely, too," she said, laughing as the pup licked her ear. She turned to her husband. "I can't decide. You pick."

"We'll have this chocolate one then," Mr Grant said.

Alex went pale.

"Actually," said Neil quickly, "that one's already promised to someone. Sorry, I should have made that clear," he mumbled awkwardly. "But the golden puppy – Candy – is just as sweet, don't you think?"

The Grants looked puzzled. "All right," Mr Grant said, putting Holly down gently and giving her a pat. "We'll take Candy instead. The colour's not important and they both seem friendly."

"Our daughter's gone away to college," Mrs Grant explained as Neil showed them out of the rescue centre. Candy was snuggled in her arms and Neil was pleased to see how well she'd taken to her new owner. "We've been lonely without her and we thought a dog would help to fill the gap."

"We're going to bring her to your dad's obedience classes," added Mr Grant as they set off across the yard to the office to sign the forms.

"I'll see you there, then," Neil called after them. He went back into the rescue centre. Alex was holding Holly in her arms. As Neil drew near, he saw that she was close to crying.

"Who's Holly promised to?" Alex asked in a wobbly voice.

"You, if you want her," said Neil gently. "But we really can't keep her for ever, Alex. The next time somebody wants her, we'll have to let her go." He picked up Cracker and made a fuss of him.

Alex nodded and blinked her tears away. "I know and I don't want her," she said decisively. "I really don't." She put Holly down in the basket and went out of the pen. "And anyway, my grandad phoned last night. He thinks he knows someone who might like one of them."

"That's great," said Neil. He put Cracker down beside his water bowl and followed Alex

78

out, shaking his head in confusion.

"I don't believe it – the thief has been here again!" Emily cried. "I left four presents under this cushion and now there are only two." Neil, Emily and Alex had decided to go back to the grotto to check on the presents and to see if they could find any clues to the identity of the thief.

Alex ran to the Christmas tree. "One's been taken from here as well," she said, dismayed.

"But how on earth did the thief know where to look?" Neil asked, mystified. He looked behind the door, and sure enough, one of the presents he'd left there had vanished as well.

They exchanged puzzled looks. "Why did he only take some of the presents again?" Emily asked.

"And this is weird, too," Neil said. "It hasn't snowed since last night but I noticed that there was only one set of footprints leading to and from the church. They must be Gavin's so where are the thief's?"

Emily and Alex followed him to the church door. Neil pointed to the tracks. "See?" he said. "Those footprints lead from the vicarage to the church and back again. And there are Jet's pawprints beside them – although he was obviously running around a bit because his tracks go all over the place."

"So the thief must have come back before last night's snowfall," Alex said.

Neil nodded. "It looks like it. Let's go and ask Gavin if he noticed anything yesterday when he locked up the church for the night."

They hurried to the vicarage and rang the bell. "Hello, you lot," said Gavin as he opened the door for them. "I was just about to go to the hospital to pick up Susie and Joshua. What can I do for you?"

"Some more presents have disappeared from the grotto," Neil said.

Gavin frowned. "You're joking!" he said. "Even after you'd hidden them? I know they were all there last night when I locked up because I checked them."

Neil looked thoughtful. "So that means they must have been taken during the night."

"But the church was locked in the night," said Gavin. "I don't understand how anyone could have got in . . . Look, I've really got to go now. I'll have to leave you to solve the mystery."

Neil, Emily, Alex and Jake made their way back to the church and examined the door for signs of a break-in. But both the door and the lock were undamaged, the windows couldn't be opened, and none of the panes of glass had been smashed.

"He must have a key then," Neil said. "It's the only explanation."

"I know! Why don't we put a sackful of paper by the door, to see if we can lure him into coming back today," suggested Alex.

"Good idea," said Neil, leading the way back to the grotto. He rummaged in the boxes of decorations. "This will do," he said, pulling out some sheets of dog-eared Christmas wrapping paper.

They filled the bag with balls of paper and Neil placed it in the doorway. "Let's hide and keep watch for a bit. The thief must have come at about this time yesterday so it's worth a try," he said. He patted Jake. "How about it, boy? Do you fancy a bit of doggy detective work."

Jake gave an eager bark and jumped up, putting his front paws on Neil's chest.

"Good for you," laughed Neil.

"Where shall we hide?" asked Emily.

They looked round. "Somewhere near the door," Neil said, "so that we can see people coming and going." He pointed to a huge, ancient gravestone that was covered in moss. "That one looks big enough to hide us all."

As they crouched down behind it, Jet trotted up. "Hello, boy," Emily said. "Have you come to help?"

Jet wagged his tail and squeezed in between Emily and Alex while Jake pressed against Neil. "At least we've got the dogs to keep us warm," Neil said in a low voice. "It's freezing out here." Though he was wearing gloves, his fingers were already numb with cold and he rubbed his hands together vigorously.

"As long as they don't make a noise and give us away," said Alex.

They settled down to watch. Out on the road a lorry drove past, puffing out a cloud of dirty exhaust fumes. Birds huddled together on the church roof and they saw an occasional shopper pass by, laden down with bulging bags. But nobody came into the churchyard.

Jake and Jet grew impatient with the long wait and wandered off to play. Neil could see them now and then, darting in and out amongst the headstones.

Time passed slowly. Grey clouds were beginning to build up overhead. "I think it's going to snow again," Alex said at last.

They all stared at the sky. "Let's give up and go home," said Emily, her teeth chattering. "I'm frozen." She came out from behind the gravestone and Alex followed her, looking relieved.

Neil stood up and stretched his cramped legs. "Yeah, I guess you're right. It doesn't look as though he's coming back today," he admitted reluctantly. He was frustrated that they hadn't been able to solve the mystery. Keeping watch at night seemed a better bet, though. Surely the thief was more likely to come back then – when he would be pretty sure that there would be no one around to see what he was up to. . .

"I'm coming back tonight," said Neil decisively.

"What, by yourself?" asked Alex.

Neil nodded.

"I'll come with you," Emily offered.

"There's no point in both of us getting frozen. And there's no point in Mum and Dad getting cross with both of us if they find out, either."

"But it'll be dark. And you'll be in a graveyard," Alex persisted.

"So?" Neil shrugged. "I've got to get to the bottom of this."

"Won't you be scared?" asked Alex.

"I'll have Jake with me," Neil pointed out. He whistled and the Border collie came running up to him obediently.

"Come on," Emily said impatiently. "If we don't go home soon, I'm going to turn into an icicle."

Snow began to fall, driven across the churchyard by an icy wind. "You won't come back tonight if it's snowing like this, will you?" Alex asked, shivering.

"Of course I will," said Neil. He wouldn't let a bit of bad weather put him off. He was determined to catch the thief, and nothing was going to stop him.

Chapter Eight

Neil's alarm clock rang at midnight. He leapt up, startled by the loudness of it, then reached out and switched it off. The house felt cold as he climbed out of bed, and he got ready quickly, shivering uncontrollably.

When he was dressed Neil picked up his torch, opened his bedroom door a crack and listened. The house was silent. Neil tiptoed along the landing and down the stairs.

Jake was asleep in the kitchen. He looked up in surprise when Neil crept in but he stood up and trotted to greet him all the same. "Good boy, Jake," Neil said, clipping on his lead. He unlocked the back door and he and Jake slipped outside.

It had been snowing all afternoon and the snow in the yard behind the house was almost knee-deep. Neil frowned, knowing that the tracks he and Jake left would give him away unless it snowed again after he got home. Still, he was determined to go ahead with his plan. He set off with his woollen hat pulled down over his ears and his collar turned up, but the icy wind still cut right through him.

Once he reached the churchyard, he hesitated. By day it had been easy to say that he wouldn't be scared, but now the moon cast an eerie glow across the snow-covered head-stones and he began to feel uneasy. He looked round anxiously. Everything was still. Tentatively, he pushed the gate open and went inside.

Neil held Jake's collar as he made his way between the graves, glad of the Border collie's company. He reached the huge gravestone near the church door, brushed away the snow from behind it and sat down to wait. The gravestone offered some protection from the wind and, with Jake pressed up against him, Neil began to warm up a little.

"Let's hope he comes soon, Jake," he whispered. Jake whined and twisted his head so that he could lick Neil's cheek.

The long, silent night wore on but nobody came. At one point Neil heard two men talking softly as they walked along the road towards the church. He stiffened and waited expectantly, but they passed by.

Neil began to feel sleepy. He shifted his position, knowing it would be dangerous to fall asleep in the cold, but it was hard to stay awake with nothing to do but stare into the darkness. And it seemed to be getting darker. Neil glanced up at the sky. Most of the stars had been blotted out by clouds and the moon was half covered too. He groaned inwardly. Surely it wasn't going to snow again. Still, at least his tracks would be covered up if it did . . .

Sure enough, snow began to fall. Neil switched on his torch, hunching over it to shield the light from anyone who might be watching, and looked at his watch. It was ten past two. He switched the torch off again and willed the thief to come. "We'll give him another quarter of an hour, Jake," he whispered. "Then we'll go home."

Jake leapt up.

"What is it, boy?" Neil reached for Jake's collar, but before he could get hold of it, the young dog dashed away around the side of the church.

"Jake!" Neil hissed. "Come back!" He scrambled up, knowing he'd got to find Jake. If he *had* heard, the thief the Border collie could be in danger. Quickly switching on his torch, Neil charged after him.

The churchyard was shadowy. Neil whirled his torch round, desperately looking for Jake, but the snow was falling fast now and the flakes got into his eyes. He brushed them away impatiently as he ran between the gravestones, swinging the torch from left to right. "Jake, where are you?" he called softly.

Suddenly Neil saw a dark shape dart behind a gravestone on the far side of the churchyard. He dashed towards it. "Jake," he hissed. "Here, boy."

Then two shapes shot out of the shadows. Neil jumped with fright, his heart hammering. But he soon relaxed as he swung the torch beam round and saw that it was Jake and Jet. Jake was all right! He must have heard Jet coming out through his dog door and run off to play!

The dogs bounded up to Neil, barking a greeting. "You gave me a scare," he scolded, patting each of them in turn. Then he clipped on Jake's lead. "Come on, you two. There's no point in hanging around here any longer. If the thief was lurking nearby, he'll have run a mile after that performance."

He led Jake to Gavin's back door and Jet trotted along behind. Neil held the dog flap open. "In you go, Jet. It's too cold for you to be out here in the middle of the night."

The black Labrador touched noses with Jake, then pushed through the dog flap. Neil let it close behind him and set off home with Jake.

*

Neil slept late the next morning. When he got downstairs Carole was clearing the breakfast table. "Morning, sleepyhead," she said.

"Morning," said Neil. She didn't look angry, he thought with relief, so she obviously didn't know about his midnight outing yet. He pushed a slice of bread into the toaster.

"Would you like some hot chocolate?" Carole asked.

"Yes, please," Neil said, yawning.

"Guess what?" Emily called, running into the kitchen. "Someone's coming from Manchester to see the puppies. A boy called Michael Todd and his mum. They know Alex's grandad."

"Oh . . . that's good, I suppose," Neil said hesitantly. He knew he should be pleased at the thought of finding a home for another of the puppies but he was worried too. What if they chose Holly? If they did, he knew Alex would be devastated. And if they chose Cracker, and Alex still refused to have Holly, then the puppy would be alone in the rescue centre for Christmas.

"Aren't you pleased?" Emily asked.

"I am really," Neil began. "It's just—"

"I know," interrupted Emily. "You think it would be best if Holly went to Alex. But it doesn't look like she'll change her mind, and time's running out."

Before Neil could reply, Sarah came rushing into the kitchen, wearing a tinsel ring on her head. "Dad's going to buy the Christmas tree later. And we're going to decorate it after tea. And I'm an angel."

Neil laughed as he spread butter on his toast. "Does that mean you're going to be good?"

"I'm always good," said Sarah indignantly. "Aren't I, Mum?"

"Most of the time," Carole said, setting Neil's mug of hot chocolate down on the worktop. "Here you are, Neil. I'll be out in Kennel Block One. Can you give me a shout when the people from Manchester get here?" She pulled on her coat and went out.

Neil looked outside, hoping she wouldn't notice the tracks he and Jake had left the night before, but the snow in the yard was deeper than ever and he knew that they would have been filled in.

Just then the front doorbell rang and Neil ran to answer it.

Alex was on the step. "Hi," she said. "I've come to see how you got on last night."

Neil shook his head. "No luck. Jake and I

waited for ages but no one showed up." As he stood aside to let her come in, a car pulled into the drive.

Alex looked round.

"We're expecting some people from Manchester," Neil explained. "They know your grandad and they want one of the puppies." He saw Alex's face cloud over. "Look – I can tell them that Holly's already promised to you, if you want. You've still got time to change your mind—"

"No, thanks," Alex interrupted, looking down at the ground.

"Come on!" said Emily, racing past them. "Oh, hello, Alex. Let's go and show the puppies to the Todds."

A woman and a boy of about eight climbed out of the car parked in the courtyard. Neil stopped to talk to them while Alex and Emily went on ahead to the rescue centre.

Just then Carole came out of Kennel Block One. "I thought I heard a car," she said, smiling. "You must be Mrs Todd. Thanks for coming. Did you have a difficult journey?"

Mrs Todd laughed wryly. "It could have been better," she said, "but we're here now. That's the main thing. Michael's been over the moon since he found out we were getting another dog."

Michael, a serious-looking boy with glasses and dark cropped hair, tugged his mother's hand. "Can we see the puppies now, Mum? Please."

"Of course you can," Carole said as she led the way to the rescue centre.

Emily and Alex were already inside. Alex was throwing a ball for Holly and the puppy was scampering after it. Cracker was lying in the basket, watching his sister's antics lazily.

Neil unfastened the pen and he and Michael went inside. Alex watched Michael anxiously as he looked from Holly to Cracker and back again. "They're lovely, aren't they?" he said. Holly charged towards him with the ball in her mouth and he stooped down to stroke her. Cracker got to his feet slowly, and padded over to meet the newcomer too.

"Shep, my last puppy, was run over," Michael said sadly, glancing at Alex and Emily. "It was terrible. I thought I'd never want another dog but I've changed my mind now. I still miss Shep but it's horrible not having a dog at home." He grinned at the girls. "Which one do you want?"

Emily glanced at Alex. Neil knew that she

was hoping Alex would tell him she'd chosen Holly – but Alex didn't say anything.

"We're not here to choose a puppy," Emily said at last. "I live here – and Alex is my friend."

Carole and Mrs Todd came towards the pen, chatting. "Of course Michael was devastated when Shep was run over," Mrs Todd was saying. "But there are so many dogs in need of good homes that it seems a shame not to have another one. Michael soon got used to the idea."

"I agree," Carole said. "Committed dog owners are hard to find."

Neil watched Alex's face. She looked guilty and confused. Perhaps seeing Michael choose a new puppy after the death of his old dog would finally help her to feel OK about adopting Holly.

"Have you chosen, Michael?" Mrs Todd asked.

Michael reached out a hand to both puppies. Cracker rolled over to have his tummy stroked. Holly darted to Alex, dropped the ball and tugged at her shoelace. "I think this black one has chosen me," Michael said, grinning. He picked up the puppy and held him against his chest. "He's great, isn't he, Mum?"

"He certainly is," agreed Mrs Todd.

Neil waited until the Todds and Carole had

gone out of the rescue centre to fill in the paperwork, then he turned to Alex. "I think Holly has chosen you, Alex."

Alex blushed. "I shouldn't have come," she said sadly. "It's not fair to Holly. She might want to live with me but I can't have her." She opened the door of the pen and started to walk away. "I won't come again. And I hope you hurry up and find somebody to take her," she called.

Emily raced after her. Neil picked Holly up. He didn't want the little puppy to be alone just yet. It would probably take her a while to adjust to life without any brothers or sisters. "That's it, then, girl," he said sadly. "I've done my best but Alex just isn't going to see that the two of you belong together."

Holly's eyes began to close. Gently Neil laid her in her basket. "We'll just have to find someone else to love you," he said with a sigh.

Chapter Nine

"Enjoy yourself, Father Christmas," Carole called from the doorstep as Bob unlocked the Range Rover. "I hope the grotto's a success." Neil, Emily, Sarah and Jake piled into the back and Alex got into the front seat.

"Enjoy myself? There's not much chance of that!" Bob replied with a grin. "I mean, think of that beard!"

"You'll be fine," Carole assured him.

"Are you sure you don't want to come, Mum?" asked Emily.

Carole shook her head. "There's too much to do here. Bev and Kate have been working flat out to prepare for our Christmas boarders, and one of us ought to be around to give them a hand."

Bob started the engine and manoeuvred the Range Rover carefully through the snow to the end of the drive. "The roads don't look too bad," he said as he turned towards Compton. "I thought we'd have to walk to the church when I got up this morning – it must have been snowing most of the night."

"It's a shame the real Father Christmas couldn't come," sighed Sarah.

"He's too busy getting ready for tomorrow night," Neil explained. "He's probably starting to load the sleigh already."

Sarah giggled with excitement. "I wish Christmas would hurry up. I can't wait to see what Father Christmas brings me." She suddenly became serious. "I won't tell anybody you're not the real Father Christmas, Dad," she promised.

"Good for you. We don't want people to be disappointed," said Bob as he pulled up outside the church. "Come on, you lot. Let's get a move on. I've still got to get changed."

They hurried to the vicarage and rang the bell. Gavin came to the door. "Hello, Bob, thanks for coming so early," he said gratefully.

He showed Bob into his study, where the Father Christmas suit was hanging, and left him to get changed. "Why don't the rest of you come into the warm kitchen?"

Jet was lying by the stove. He lifted his head and looked at them as they came in, then flopped down again. "He doesn't look too lively," Neil said, crouching down to pat him.

Gavin frowned. "He's been a bit low lately."

Sarah went to stroke the black Labrador. "He's really excited about seeing Father Christmas," she said. Then she added in a whisper, "He doesn't know it's only Dad dressed up." Jake trotted over to her, and lay down beside Jet with his head resting on the older dog's back.

"Oh, I nearly forgot," said Neil suddenly. "We've brought a few posters with us advertising the last of our Labrador puppies. Would you mind if we put them up in the grotto?"

"Not at all," Gavin said.

Susie, Gavin's wife, came into the kitchen. "I thought I heard voices," she said, beaming round at them.

"Hello," said Emily. "How's Joshua?"

"He's fine – he's asleep upstairs. Would you

all like to see him?"

"Oh yes, please!" Emily said enthusiastically.

Neil couldn't see why anyone would get so excited about seeing a new baby. If Gavin and Susie had a new puppy, that would be different . . .

As they went out of the kitchen, Jake got up to follow them. "You stay here, Jake," Neil commanded.

"It's all right," said Susie. "Jake can come too, if he likes. Joshua's got to get used to dogs."

"Come on then, Jake," Neil said. "But be quiet. You'll be in trouble if you wake the baby."

Susie led the way upstairs. "He's in here," she said softly. A double bed occupied most of the floor space but there was a wicker crib standing beside it. "Go in and have a look at him," said Susie. "I'm just going to run myself a bath."

They crept into the room and gathered round the crib. The baby was fast asleep, his downy blond hair standing up in wisps and his tiny hands clutching his quilt. "Isn't he lovely?" Alex whispered.

"I wish we could take him home," said Sarah. Suddenly, Neil heard a rustling and

crunching sound behind him. Leaving the girls
to admire Joshua, he turned quickly, worried
that Jake was up to mischief. The Border collie
was lying half under Gavin and Susie's bed. He
seemed to be chewing something.

"What have you got there, Jake?" Neil hissed.
He bent down to see, then drew back in
astonishment. Jake was chewing a rubber bone
wrapped in paper. Neil recognized it. It was one
of the presents from the church.

"Where did you get that? Come out of there."
As Jake slunk out from under the bed, Neil saw
that there were more presents there. Hardly

able to believe his eyes, he bent down to have a proper look. There was no doubt about it. The missing presents were piled under the vicar's bed!

Neil took the rubber bone away from Jake, then sat back on his heels to think. Surely Gavin hadn't stolen the presents himself. But what other explanation could there be? The last place a thief would think to hide them would be in the vicarage.

He looked round to see if anyone else had noticed but Emily, Sarah and Alex were still peering at the baby.

Just then Jet came into the bedroom. To Neil's surprise, he was carrying one of the presents from the grotto in his mouth. He squirmed under the bed, deposited the present on the pile and wriggled out again. Then he lay down beside Neil, looking rather pleased with himself.

"Jet's the thief!" Neil cried.

"What?" said Emily, whirling round in astonishment. "He can't be!"

"He is." Neil showed her the heap of presents. "He just brought one in and added it to the pile."

"The baby's waking up," Alex said.

Neil's hand flew to his mouth. "I'd forgotten all about him."

Joshua began to cry and Susie rushed into the bedroom and picked him up.

"Sorry," Neil apologized. "It was my fault. I'd just discovered what had happened to your missing presents and I forgot that I had to be quiet."

"What do you mean?" asked Gavin, coming into the room.

Neil pointed to the bed. "They're here – Jake found them. It looks like Jet's been taking them all along."

Gavin bent down and peered under the bed. He ruffled Jet's fur. "What on earth have you been up to, Jet?" He pulled out a few of the presents. "They look all right," he said. "I should be able to take the second lot I bought back to the shop and get a refund."

"The dogs will get more exciting presents, too, rather than just dog treats," Neil said.

"And the grotto will make some money for the church hall roof repairs," said Emily.

Gavin smiled. "Yes, it will. And it's all thanks to you, Neil, and to Jake."

"How did Jet take the presents during the night, though?" asked Alex. "The church is closed then."

Gavin looked thoughtful. "Well, he came with me when I went to lock up. I was there for a while, sorting a few things out, so I suppose he could have taken them then. He must have gone backwards and forwards from the church hall to the house to steal all those presents, though – and without me even noticing."

"We saw that he'd left lots of tracks in the snow," Emily said.

"And being a dog, he'd be able to sniff the presents out," Neil added, "even after we'd hidden them. Does he usually take things?"

Gavin shook his head. "Not that I know of."

"So why has he suddenly started it now?" asked Neil, thinking out loud.

"He's been a bit moody and depressed lately," Gavin said. "And I've been feeling bad because I haven't had time to walk him much."

"He's probably been stealing to get your attention then," Neil said knowledgeably. "He must feel a bit left out. Dogs often feel like that when there's a new baby in the family."

"Oh, poor Jet!" cried Susie. She called him and the Labrador trotted eagerly to her. "We still love you, boy," she said, rubbing the side of his head with her free hand. The big dog's tail wagged happily.

"Let's get the presents out," Gavin said, lying down and reaching under the bed.

Suddenly they heard a voice from downstairs. "Ho ho ho!"

"It's Father Christmas!" cried Sarah.

"It's Dad," Neil laughed. They all carried an armful of presents downstairs. Bob was standing in the hall, dressed in his Father Christmas outfit. His face was almost hidden by a white beard, which was even bushier than his real one. "How do I look?" he asked.

Jake sat at Bob's feet and gazed up at him with his head on one side, as though he couldn't work out why Bob was dressed in such strange clothes. Neil burst out laughing.

"It's not that bad, is it?" Bob asked.

"Worse!" Neil grinned. He put the presents down on the hall table. "I wouldn't want to be seen in an outfit like that."

"It wouldn't fit you anyway," Sarah said, taking Bob's hand protectively and scowling at Neil.

"But the elf suit would," said Bob. He turned to Gavin. "That elf suit you've got hanging in your study looks exactly the right size for Neil."

Neil stared at his dad in horror. "No way!" he said. "I'm not dressing up as an elf for anybody."

"But Gavin got it out specially for you," Bob persisted, with a twinkle in his eye.

Neil shook his head firmly. "Absolutely not!"

Emily, Alex and Sarah laughed. "Make him wear it, Dad," begged Emily. "Then we can take a picture of him and hang it up at home for everyone to see."

Alex glanced at her watch. "The grotto's meant to be opening in a few minutes," she reminded them. "Do you think we ought to get over to the church hall?"

They went out into the snow, with Jake and Jet bounding ahead of them. A queue of people and dogs were waiting outside. They cheered when they saw Father Christmas. Neil recognized most of them. He stopped to speak to Doctor Harvey and to make a fuss of his two dogs, Finn and Sandy. Mr Hamley, Neil's head teacher, was in the queue too, with Dotty his wayward Dalmatian. Neil wished he had time to greet all of the dogs but Gavin was obviously in a hurry to open the grotto.

Bob went into the church hall and sat on the tinsel-covered chair behind the screen. Emily arranged the presents on either side of him – one pile for children and another for dogs – while Alex switched on the fairy lights and Neil hung up the posters with Holly's picture on them. "Let's hope these do the trick," he said to himself.

"Are you ready?" Gavin asked, sticking his head round the door.

"I think so," said Neil. He peered behind the screen. "Good luck, Dad."

"Thanks," Bob said, tugging at his white beard. "This thing is driving me mad already and I haven't even started yet." He chuckled. "I don't know how I let myself get talked into this."

Emily and Alex positioned themselves at the edge of the screen, ready to take the money.

"Ladies, gentlemen, children and dogs," Gavin said from the other side of the door. "I declare this Christmas grotto open." He flung the door wide and people began to flock inside, admiring the Christmas tree and the decorations. A queue quickly formed by the screen and Emily and Alex began to collect the money.

Sarah was working her way around the room, stroking all the dogs and saying hello to schoolfriends. Neil couldn't help smiling as he watched her – she looked ready to burst at having to keep their Father Christmas's true identity a secret.

Looking round the room, he could see excitement on lots of faces. *Only two more days to go!* he thought. Then he spotted the poster of Holly and his happiness evaporated. It wouldn't be much of a Christmas for the Labrador puppy unless they could find her a home.

Chapter Ten

The crowd was finally thinning when Gavin appeared with a tray of tea. "Could you take one of these in to Father Christmas, please, Neil?"

"Right." Neil went behind the screen and waited until Bob's visitor had finished, then he handed him the cup.

"Just what I need!" Bob croaked. "I've said 'Ho ho ho' so many times that I've almost lost my voice."

"How's it going, apart from that?" asked Neil.

Bob fiddled with the white beard. "I'm so hot I feel as though I've been cooked, and this wretched beard is tickling my nose. But I've patted lots of friendly dogs, seen lots of cheerful faces and heard about all the things the children of Compton would like for Christmas. I've nearly run out of presents, though. How many people are still waiting to see me?"

"Only four or five," Neil said. "But one of them is Mrs Jepson. Sugar and Spice are really looking forward to seeing you," he added, laughing.

"Oh no! Spare me!"

"I'll leave you to it," said Neil, with a grin.

A young couple were looking at one of the posters of Holly when he came out from behind the screen. A red setter was sitting listlessly at their feet, her head drooping and her eyes half closed.

Neil went over and crouched down beside her. He held out a hand to her. "Hello, girl. What's up?"

The dog sniffed him half-heartedly, and he patted her gently.

"Your dog doesn't look too happy," Neil said to its owners, standing up.

The couple turned. "I know," the woman said anxiously. "Poor Topsy. We've got a vet's appointment today but a friend of ours thinks she might be lonely." She pointed to the poster. "We've been thinking of getting a puppy to keep her company. That one looks perfect."

Neil hesitated before he replied. He was still secretly hoping that Alex would change her mind. But he knew that they'd run out of time – Holly needed a home now. "I'm the person you need to speak to about the puppy," Neil told the couple eventually. "My name's Neil Parker and I live at King Street Kennels. Holly's a great little dog – really friendly. Do you want to meet her?"

"Yes, we'll go straight away, if that's OK," the man said enthusiastically. "It'll be nice to have a puppy in the house again at Christmas." Neil gave them directions to the kennels and they hurried out of the hall, with Topsy trailing behind them.

As soon as they had gone, Neil raced over to Emily. "That couple are going to have a look at Holl—" He broke off quickly as Alex came out from behind the screen.

She stared at him in shock. "Do you mean they're going to adopt her?" she said in a wobbly voice.

"Yes, I'm afraid so," said Neil, looking at his feet.

Alex's eyes filled with tears. "No! We've got to stop them! Holly's *my* dog. I want her to live with *me*."

"But why didn't you say something before?" asked Neil, exasperated. "We gave you so many chances to change your mind! It's too late now."

"I didn't feel like this before," sobbed Alex. "I mean, I liked Holly but it seemed wrong to want another dog – after Daisy."

Emily smiled sadly at Alex. "There'll be other dogs at the rescue centre. You can always have one of those."

Alex sobbed harder than ever. "I don't want any other dog. I only want Holly." She gripped Neil's arm. "We've got to stop those people. We've got to tell them Holly's already got an owner."

Neil shook his head sadly. "I'm sorry, Alex," he said, "but it's too late. There's nothing we can do now. If they want her, then she's theirs."

Neil stared gloomily out of the window of the Range Rover as Bob drove back to King Street Kennels. Compton was ablaze with coloured lights but Neil hardly noticed them. He was too upset about what had happened.

Beside him, Alex and Emily sat in miserable silence. Even Sarah was subdued.

As Bob reached the kennels, a car turned out of the drive. Neil recognized the young couple inside it – the people he'd spoken to at the grotto. He peered into the car and caught a glimpse of Holly sitting next to the red setter on the back seat.

Alex had seen the puppy too. "It's Holly!" she cried, and burst into tears again.

As Bob parked the car, Carole came out to meet them, smiling. "Holly's gone," she said cheerfully. "Mr and Mrs Biggs have taken her. They seem really nice. Apparently their other dog—" She stopped when she saw Alex's miserable face. "What on earth's wrong?" she asked.

"Alex has realized that she wants Holly, after

all," explained Emily.

"Oh dear, you poor thing," sighed Carole. "Let's go inside and talk about it." She led Alex into the kitchen.

Neil and Emily followed a few moments later, and found Alex sitting at the kitchen table with a box of tissues and a glass of Coke in front of her. They decided that it was best to leave her with their mum, and went through into the sitting room. The Christmas tree stood in the window, glittering brightly.

"It doesn't feel like Christmas any more," Emily said gloomily.

"This whole thing is my fault," said Neil, slumping into a chair beside the fire.

"No, it isn't," Emily said. "You tried to get Alex to take Holly. We both did."

"But I told those people how great Holly is too." Neil seized a cushion and thumped it angrily. "Why didn't I say she'd already got a home? Then Alex could have had her."

Emily sat on the arm of his chair. "Alex insisted she didn't want her," she pointed out. "And we could hardly have kept Holly in the rescue centre for ever, while we waited for Alex to change her mind. Especially not at Christmas."

Sarah came into the room and stood by the Christmas tree, touching the baubles and setting them swinging so that they shone in the firelight. "Why's everybody so grumpy?" she demanded. "It's nearly Christmas."

Neil shrugged. All the excitement he'd been feeling about Christmas had evaporated. Holly and Alex would never be together now and there was nothing Neil could do about it.

Neil woke early on Christmas Eve. He lay staring up at his bedroom ceiling, trying to recapture the Christmas spirit he'd felt at the grotto, but images of Holly and of Alex's tear-streaked face kept crowding into his head.

He decided to get up and take Jake for a run. As usual, the Border collie was eager to go out, so the two of them set off for the ridgeway.

The ground was still thick with snow and the rising sun set it sparkling as though it were scattered with diamonds. It was a fantastic morning, but Neil couldn't really enjoy it – not while his head ached with the misery of knowing Holly and Alex were parted for good.

Neil let Jake off the lead and watched him racing back and forth, throwing up clouds of loose snow at every step.

They climbed steadily. By the time they reached the top of the hill, the sun was up and Compton lay below them, the snowy roofs and gardens looking strangely out of place against the brilliant blue sky behind.

A figure appeared on a path a little way away. Neil recognized her and his heart sank. He'd come here to try to forget about Alex for a while and here she was, walking slowly towards him.

Alex glanced up and saw him. She looked pale and miserable. "Sorry about yesterday," she said.

"How are you feeling?" Neil asked.

She shrugged. "Pretty awful, actually. But I know it was my own stupid fault . . . Look, I really can't stop and talk – Mum and Dad will be wondering where I am." She turned away. "Have a good Christmas."

Neil watched her walk away from him, head down and shoulders drooping. He wished there was something he could do or say that would cheer her up. But he knew it was hopeless.

"Neil!" Emily was dashing up the hill towards him.

"What's wrong?" Neil called.

"Nothing. Well . . . I don't know. Mum and Dad sent me to fetch Alex," Emily panted.

"Why?" asked Neil.

"They wouldn't say," said Emily. "But they looked pretty pleased."

Neil shook his head. "I can't imagine what they could do to cheer her up. I've just seen her and she looks really upset."

"Well, you never know. Go and get her – and hurry up!"

"OK," Neil agreed reluctantly. He caught up with Alex near the path that led into her road. "Wait!" he called.

Alex turned.

"You've got to come to the kennels with me. Mum and Dad need to see you."

"I expect they want me to look at another dog." Alex shook her head. "It's kind of them but I'm not interested." She turned to go.

"Please," Neil said, catching her arm. "They wouldn't have sent Emily to find you if it wasn't important."

Alex shrugged. "OK. But it's a waste of time."

They hurried down to the kennels. Carole and Bob were waiting for them in the kitchen. "What's going on?" Neil asked. He fetched a towel and rubbed Jake's fur dry.

"You'll see." Bob winked at him, then placed a plate of hot, buttered toast on the table. "Tuck into this while you're waiting."

Just then Neil heard a car driving into the yard. Carole ran to the front door and opened it. "They're here!" she cried.

"Who's here?" Neil demanded, standing up.

"Just wait and see," said Bob.

Neil glanced at Emily, hoping that she could explain what was going on, but she looked just as mystified as he felt. They heard Carole inviting somebody to come inside, then a dog's claws clicking along the hall. A moment later, Holly scampered into the kitchen, her tail wagging wildly. She spotted Alex and darted straight to her. Alex stared at the Labrador, her face clouded with uncertainty.

Holly jumped up and Alex bent down to stroke her.

"What's going on?" Neil asked. "Why's Holly here?"

Carole came into the room with Mr and Mrs Biggs, the couple who had adopted Holly. "Mrs Biggs rang earlier," said Carole, "while you were out with Jake."

"That's right," Mr Biggs said. "We took Topsy to the vet last night and it turns out that she's pregnant."

"Pregnant?" Neil repeated. "Of course! That's

why she was looking a bit low."

"Yes, I suppose we should have thought of it before, really," said Mr Biggs rather sheepishly.

Suddenly Neil understood what this meant. "So, I suppose you can't really keep Holly now?" he asked tentatively, glancing across at Alex's hopeful face.

"Not really, no. We felt terrible about having to bring Holly back," Mrs Biggs went on. "But we just won't be able to manage her when we've got a litter of pups to see to. And when we rang to explain what had happened, your mum told us that somebody else wanted Holly anyway." She beamed at Alex. "I can see you're already very fond of her. And she obviously loves you."

Alex's eyes shone with joy. She swept the puppy into her arms and hugged her tightly. "Oh Holly, I can hardly believe it," she cried. "Thank you for bringing her back. This is going to be the best Christmas ever!"

The Morgans and Holly came to King Street Kennels for Christmas dinner. As everyone sat down at the table, Neil looked round happily. It had turned out to be a perfect day.

He looked across the kitchen to where Bob was carving the turkey. Jake and Holly were sitting at his feet, watching hopefully in case he dropped a piece of meat. Mr and Mrs Morgan and Alex seemed happy and relaxed. Through the kitchen window, Neil could see snow falling gently.

"I'm glad you could all come today," Carole said. She filled everyone's glass. "As soon as Bob brings the turkey over, I think we should drink a toast."

They waited expectantly as Bob carried the turkey carefully to the table, stepping over the eager dogs.

Carole raised her glass. "To Alex and Holly.

It's great to see them back together again. And here's to a merry Christmas for all of us."

Neil grinned as they chinked glasses. He looked down at Holly, who was leaning contentedly against Alex's leg, and his smile broadened. For a while it had looked as though this Christmas would be terrible, but in the end it was turning out to be one of the best he'd ever had.

Look out for Puppy Patrol® No. 33:

Homeward Bound

A doggy stowaway!

A canal holiday is the perfect treat for the Parker family – a whole week without puppy problems. But there's a secret stowaway hiding in their boat – with four legs and a loud bark!

Their doggy guest loves the water – but she can't live on the boat for ever. Can Neil and Emily find her a home on dry land?

PUPPY PATROL® titles available from Macmillan Children's Books

The prices shown below are correct at the time of going to press. However, Macmillan Publishers reserve the right to show new retail prices on covers which may differ from those previously advertised.

JENNY DALE

1.	Teacher's Pet	£2.99	21.	The Puppy Project	£2.99
2.	Big Ben	£2.99	22.	Superdog!	£2.99
3.	Abandoned!	£2.99	23.	Sherlock's Home	£2.99
4.	Double Trouble	£2.99	24.	Forever Sam	£2.99
5.	Star Paws	£2.99	25.	Milly's Triumph	£2.99
6.	Tug of Love	£2.99	26.	The Snow Dog	£2.99
7.	Saving Skye	£2.99	27.	Boomerang Bob	£2.99
8.	Tuff's Luck	£2.99	28.	Willow's Wood	£2.99
9.	Red Alert	£2.99	29.	Dognapped!	£2.99
10.	The Great Escape	£2.99	30.	Puppy Power!	£2.99
11.	Perfect Puppy	£2.99	31.	Two's Company	£2.99
12.	Sam & Delilah	£2.99	32.	Digger's Treasure	£2.99
13.	The Sea Dog	£2.99	33.	Homeward Bound	£2.99
14.	Puppy School	£2.99	34.	The Puppy Express	£2.99
15.	A Winter's Tale	£2.99	35.	Holly's Wish	£2.99
16.	Puppy Love	£2.99			
17.	Best of Friends	£2.99			
18.	King of the Castle	£2.99			
19.	Posh Pup	£2.99			
20.	Charlie's Choice	£2.99			

All Macmillan titles can be ordered at your local bookshop or are available by post from:

**Book Service by Post
PO Box 29, Douglas, Isle of Man IM99 1BQ**

Credit cards accepted. For details:
Telephone: 01624 675137
Fax: 01624 670923
E-mail: bookshop@enterprise.net

Free postage and packing in the UK.
Overseas customers: add £1 per book (paperback)
and £3 per book (hardback).